STICKNEY-FOREST VIEW LIBRARY DISTRICT

3 1803 00166 4580

W9-AAX-296

Baby Bear Eats the Night

by **Anthony Pearson**

illustrated by **Bonnie Leick**

Marshall Cavendish Children

Text copyright © 2012 by Anthony Pearson
Illustrations copyright © 2012 by Bonnie Leick

All rights reserved

Marshall Cavendish Corporation
99 White Plains Road
Tarrytown, NY 10591
www.marshallcavendish.us/kids

Library of Congress Cataloging-in-Publication Data
Pearson, Anthony, 1980-
Baby Bear eats the night / by Anthony Pearson ;
illustrated by Bonnie Leick. — 1st ed.
p. cm.
Summary: When Baby Bear goes to bed, the shadows
and sounds frighten him, so he comes up with a plan
to get rid of the night.
ISBN 978-0-7614-6103-6 (hardcover) —
ISBN 978-0-7614-6104-3 (ebook)
[1. Fear of the dark—Fiction. 2. Night—Fiction.
3. Bears—Fiction. 4. Animals—Fiction.] I. Leick,
Bonnie, ill. II. Title.
PZ7.P31667Bab 2012   [E]—dc23   2011016342

The illustrations are rendered in watercolor with
some line work done in colored pencil.
Book design by Vera Soki
Editor: Robin Benjamin
Printed in Malaysia (T)
First edition
10 9 8 7 6 5 4 3 2 1

mc Marshall Cavendish
Children

To Liz, for always believing
To Kristen, for constantly reading
To Ella, for simply being
To Robin, for deftly editing

This book exists for you and because of you
—A.P.

For Tommy
—B.L.

Mama Bear put Baby Bear down to sleep. Their cave was warm, and Baby Bear's bed was soft. Baby Bear should've gone right to sleep, but he couldn't. . . .

At night, when the shadows grew long, sounds became scary. Baby Bear could hear snapping branches and feet skittering through bushes.

Who could sleep with so many things out there in the dark?

So Baby Bear slipped out of the cave and went into the forest alone. He was afraid, but he had a plan. He was going to get rid of the night!

The night was a blanket that covered
everything.
The ground was covered by night.
The trees were covered by night.
Even the big lake was covered by night.

Baby Bear climbed the tallest tree he could find. With a swift stroke of his claws, he cut a line into the sky. A flap of night waved in the breeze. Baby Bear grabbed it and made his way to the ground.

The night came down in a dark, dark ribbon.

Baby Bear sat with the night in his paws. It felt cool and weighed almost nothing.

"This is going to be easy," he thought.

Baby Bear was going to eat the night!

He opened his mouth and began to chew. . . .

Along came Field Mouse. "Bear, what are you doing?"

"I'm eating the night," said Baby Bear.

"You can't do that! Field mice need the night to hide. Forest animals love to eat mice, so we move around at night."

"You'll have to find a new way to hide," said Baby Bear.

Field Mouse scurried off. Baby Bear kept eating.

Firefly landed on Baby Bear's nose. "Hullo, Bear. What are you doing?"

"I'm eating the night."

"You can't do that! Fireflies need the night so our light can be seen! That is how we talk to each other and how we keep other animals away."

"I'm sure you'll find new ways to do that," said Baby Bear.

Firefly flew off. Baby Bear kept eating.

Bat flew by. "Bear, are you eating
the night?" he shouted.

"Yes, I am."

"But what about bats? Our eyes are
designed to see in the dark, so we fly
at night."

Baby Bear shrugged. "You can find
nighttime somewhere else."

"Not if you eat all of it!" said Bat,
flying off with a screech.

Baby Bear thought, "If I get any
more visitors, I'll never finish!"
He started shoving pawfuls of
night into his mouth.
He ate the clouds, the stars, and
the moon.

While it was true that Baby Bear was eating the night, what was left behind was not the day. There wasn't any sunlight or bright blue sky. There wasn't any sound of birds singing. There was just a white nothingness that hurt his eyes.

Field Mouse, Firefly, and Bat woke up Mama Bear. When she saw what Baby Bear was doing, she couldn't believe her eyes. "Baby Bear, why are you eating the night?"

"Because I'm scared of the dark!" Baby Bear cried.

"My sweet cub, did you know that bears need the night? We search for food at night, and the dark helps keep us safe from hunters."

"I didn't know that," said Baby Bear. "But what should I do? I ate so much of it already."

"We'll help you," said Mama Bear.

She nuzzled Baby Bear's ears. Then Field Mouse tickled his feet, and Firefly flapped her wings against his nose. Baby Bear giggled, and then he coughed. And then, at last, came a tremendous burp that shook the trees and set the whole night free.

Bat flew around the sky, holding the
night ribbon and putting everything
back in its proper place—

the clouds, the stars, and the moon.

"I'm sorry that I didn't listen," said Baby Bear. "I'm sorry that I was afraid."

Mama Bear smiled. "The shadows at night do grow long and the sounds can be scary, but many sounds are from our friends and we need those shadows."

Baby Bear looked up at the twinkling lights. He listened to the peaceful sounds. And he knew that the night can be a bear's friend, too.